The Dolls' Christmas

The Dolls' Christmas

BY TASHA TUDOR

Henry Z. Walck, Inc.
New York

E
TUD

Library of Congress Catalog Card Number: 59-12744
ISBN: 0-8098-1026-3 (Cloth)
ISBN: 0-8098-2912-6 (Paperback)

10 9 8 7 6 5 4 3 2
MANUFACTURED IN THE UNITED STATES OF AMERICA

The Dolls' Christmas

To all the
Children
and Dolls
who come
to the
Christmas
Party

and to
Rosabelle
for
helping
out

*O*NCE upon a time there were two very old dolls who lived with two little girls in an old red house. The dolls' names were Sethany Ann and Nicey Melinda. The girls' names were Laura and Efner.

Sethany Ann was French and very elegant, Nicey Melinda wasn't elegant but she was full of character. She had the brightest eyes of blue glass and a nose quite worn down with generations of loving and scrubbing.

The dolls were extremely fortunate for they had a house all their own, which was named Pumpkin House.

Sethany and Nicey were not doll-house dolls at all, they were large dolls, over a foot tall. What was so wonderful about Pumpkin House was that it was the right size for large dolls. It took up the side of a room and even turned the corner. Efner had to stand on a chair to reach the second floor. There was a kitchen, two bedrooms, a bathroom, a parlor, a dining-room and a front hall and a conservatory with real pots of plants in it and a live turtle named Ezekiel. The house had everything two dolls could need from an iron stove in the kitchen to a complete set of china in the dining-room cupboards. It even had electric lights and a handsome horsehair sofa.

Every year at Christmas Sethany and Nicey had a dinner party and a Christmas tree of their own, and after dinner they had a marionette show given especially in their honor, to which they invited all their friends. Laura and Efner sent out the invitations on doll-size notepaper by Sparrow Post.

This is what the invitation said:

Miss Sethany Ann
and
Miss Nicey Melinda
request the pleasure
of your company
at a
Marionette Show
On Christmas Day
at
Candelight
at The Red House

Of course there had to be a great deal of preparation for such a party. Two days before the party Laura and Efner dressed Nicey and Sethany in their warmest clothes and took them to the woods to get the dolls' Christmas tree.

When they came home they had tea to warm themselves, and then decorated the tree. They hung it with silver nutmegs and golden pears and bright balls of many colors. They made a paper chain and cornucopias, and wound it round and round with tinsel.

The day after gathering greens the children's cousins arrived for the holidays. One of the cousins had a doll named Lucy, she was Sethany's and Nicey's best friend. She was taken to the spare room of Pumpkin House where she and Nicey and Sethany spent a happy morning talking about many things. Dolls do talk, you know.

In the afternoon the dolls put on their aprons and came to the kitchen to help with the party preparations. There were cookies to be cut with thimbles, small pies to be rolled, a pan of tiny biscuits and a small mold of jelly to be made. The dolls felt quite tired when everything was finally finished and put away. They went to bed in expectation of tomorrow.

After opening their stockings the dolls spent the day quietly until four when they were washed, powdered and dressed in their best clothes. Laura cut a bouquet of rose geraniums for Sethany to hold, and pinned some in her hair, too. The dolls looked very beautiful.

Lucy, Nicey and Sethany came down as the tall clock struck half-past three. Dinner was to be served in the parlor of the red house because there wasn't room in the Pumpkin House for all the guests. Just three dolls had been invited as the dinner service was for six only. Their names were Henrietta, Meg and Trilby, and they were waiting in the hall. They all went in to dinner.

The dolls awoke to find three stockings hanging on the mantelpiece. They were filled with tiny presents and topped off with doll-sized candy canes.

The dolls awoke to find three stockings hanging on the mantelpiece. They were filled with tiny presents and topped off with doll-sized candy canes.

After opening their stockings the dolls spent the day quietly until four when they were washed, powdered and dressed in their best clothes. Laura cut a bouquet of rose geraniums for Sethany to hold, and pinned some in her hair, too. The dolls looked very beautiful.

Lucy, Nicey and Sethany came down as the tall clock struck half-past three. Dinner was to be served in the parlor of the red house because there wasn't room in the Pumpkin House for all the guests. Just three dolls had been invited as the dinner service was for six only. Their names were Henrietta, Meg and Trilby, and they were waiting in the hall. They all went in to dinner.

What a delightful sight met their eyes! On one side of the room stood the dolls' tree, completely surrounded by presents. In the middle of the room was the bread board, spread with a lacy cloth. There were four candles in silver candlesticks and a centerpiece of geraniums and parsley. Tiny place cards told them where to sit. The boys of the family played butler and served the dinner.

There were three courses beginning with soup and ending with ice cream and champagne in a doll-size bottle, only it was ginger ale. They all enjoyed themselves immensely.

After dinner the dolls sat about the tree and opened their presents. I couldn't possibly tell you all that they received for that would take too long. By candlelight time all was in readiness for the marionette show. The family were dressed in old fashioned clothes. The children and dolls sat waiting for their guests.

The first to arrive were Tedward and Edward Bear, Effilly Elephant, Trilby and Mr. Kitty. Then came Lily, Oliver Twist, Meg, Henrietta and several others.

When everyone was assembled the candles were blown out and the play began. It was *Little Red Riding Hood.*

Everyone had the best time, at least everyone but Trilby who was sat upon for half the performance, and Mr. Kitty who fell to the floor in a fright at the sight of the wicked wolf. When the play was over they all ate cookies and the children sang carols around the big Christmas tree. Then the guests went home, all but Effilly who was forgotten. He spent the night under the table and had an interesting discussion with some mice about cake crumbs compared to peanuts.

In Pumpkin House the dolls went to bed. "I think," said Nicey, "that Christmas is the most magic time in all the year, not just for the pretty things you get, but for the feeling inside you of what a good place the world is to live in. I should know for I have seen one hundred and ten Christmases!"

```
E       Tudor, Tasha
TUD     The doll's Christmas
```

LIBRARY
U. S. COAST GUARD

BORROWERS.—Officers, cadets, enlisted personnel, and civilian employees, together with their families, may borrow books.

SIGNING FOR BOOK.—Each book taken from the library must be signed for on the book card.

TIME KEPT.—Books may be kept for 14 days and renewed for 14 days when necessary.

CLASS USE.—Books used by instructors for class work may be kept for a semester, provided arrangements are made with the librarian.

RETURNING BOOKS.—When returning a borrowed book always leave it on the library desk.

DEPT. OF TRANSP., USCG
CG-9688 (Rev. 6-67)

PREVIOUS EDITION MAY BE USED   ☆GPO 614-842